ROSLYN, THE RELUCTANT
RATTLESNAKE

Roslyn, The Reluctant Rattlesnake

THOMAS FULLMER

Library of Congress Control Number:		2020901212
ISBN:	Hardcover	978-1-7960-8557-0
	Softcover	978-1-7960-8558-7
	eBook	978-1-7960-8565-5

Print information available on the last page.

Rev. date: 01/30/2020

To order additional copies of this book, contact:
Xlibris
1-888-795-4274
www.Xlibris.com
Orders@Xlibris.com
808470

Roslyn the rattlesnake filled the forest folk with fear. She would shake her rattle so they would know not to come near. Roslyn didn't want to poison any new forest friend. Roslyn was a rattlesnake, created for that end. When forest creatures came near and didn't flee, Roslyn swallowed them whole somewhat reluctantly. None would come near to even say "Hi!" So Roslyn became lonelier and lonelier as the days drifted by.

Roslyn went weeks on end with nothing to eat until her hunger grew and she would hunt for meat. Roslyn would lay in her coils until a mouse, gopher, or bird fluttered by. Then she'd shoot forth her fangs without a single cry.

Roslyn tried to make friends with a chipmunk named Cali. But when Cali came close, Roslyn's rattling made Cali flee. She knew if Cali had come too close, she would have been lunch. It made Roslyn feel guilty and hurt her a bunch. How would Roslyn ever end her extreme loneliness? Any friend she met became dinner, she had to confess.

One day, Roslyn slithered down by a pond. She came here often to drink at a place of which she was fond. She looked across the pond, and what did she see? A rather large rattlesnake who was handsome and brawny. The two skirted the pond and met across a stream. He smiled at Roslyn as she started to beam. He hissed and smiled. Roslyn's heart went all aflutter. She tried to hiss "Hi" but could only stutter.

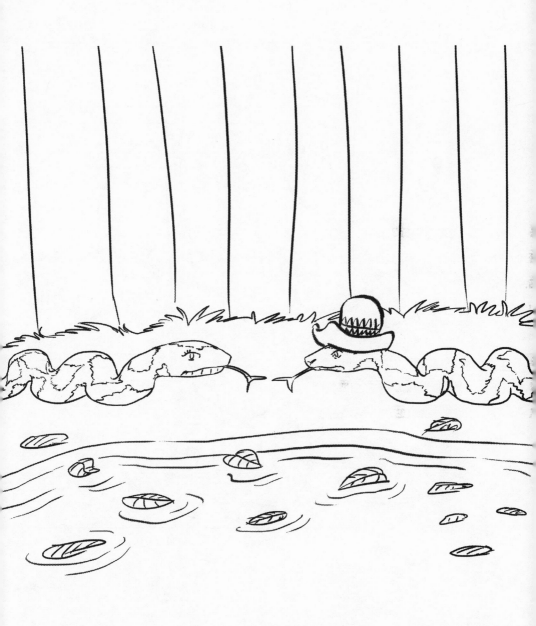

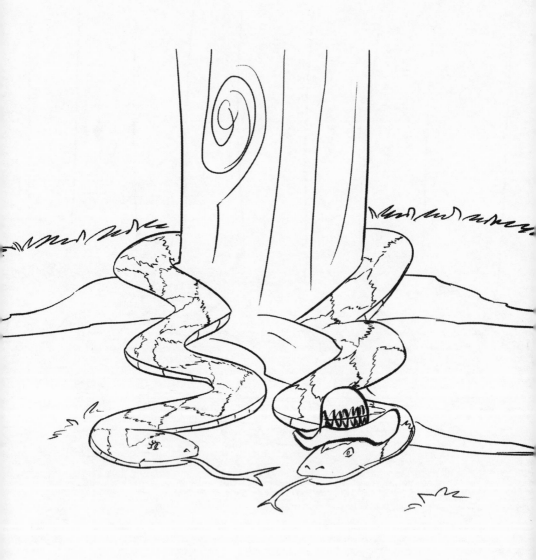

The rattlesnake hissed, "Hi! My name is Rico! Your diamond scales are so pretty. Come on, let's go!"

Roslyn blushed red as a raspberry but didn't retreat. She liked this new rattlesnake and thought Rico was so neat. "My name is Roslyn. Will you be my friend? I've been looking for someone to make my loneliness end."

So Roslyn and Rico slithered off between the old oak trees. She found that talking to Rico was such a breeze. They hissed and touched as they slithered across the forest floor. Roslyn came to believe she'd be lonely no more.

Roslyn and Rico hunted to swallow gophers whole. She forgot her reluctance as her belly started to grow. Rico found a nest of ducklings and gobbled them up. He saved one for Roslyn on which she could sup. Roslyn followed Rico over rocky crags and through grassy glens. They were more than just companions; they were the best of friends.

Rico was kind and funny and made Roslyn laugh. Rico did so many kind deeds on Roslyn's behalf. Rico knew forest lore and taught Roslyn so much. She loved to be with him and feel his scaly touch.

One day, Roslyn rested while Rico hunted in a field of clover. She had fallen asleep with much to think over. When Roslyn woke up, her Rico was gone. He broke Roslyn's heart because only to Rico she was drawn. She couldn't admit that her time with Rico was finished. Roslyn couldn't imagine how her pain could ever be diminished. Rico's absence weighed so heavily upon Roslyn's lonely soul. She didn't realize how his gift within her would grow.

Roslyn left the field and searched through the forest instead. She feared a hawk had eaten Rico and he was now dead. She came to accept that her only friend was now gone. Was there no one in the world she could ever rely on?

Roslyn wandered the forest, lost and forlorn. She was very sad with Rico to mourn. She slithered aimlessly, ignoring the birds and the bees. Roslyn didn't see a nearby quail that escaped into the trees. She didn't realize she was starving to death. She was so very lonely and could barely draw breath.

Roslyn went into a burrow to find rest but found Weasel instead. The look in Weasel's eyes told her he wanted her dead. Roslyn shook her rattle and backed out of the burrow. She wished Rico was there to play her hero. Coiled on the ground, she hissed and bared her fangs wide. Roslyn saw no place to escape to, no place to hide.

Weasel screeched as he danced round and round.
He was so very fierce and made such an awful sound.
Weasel darted in and out, his sharp claws slashing.
Roslyn dodged from side to side, her fangs flashing.

She slithered sideways to the edge of a crag. She dodged Weasel with a zig and a zag. Roslyn heard a rapid's roar far down below. How would she survive? She just didn't know.

Weasel darted in to finish Roslyn off. He swiped at Roslyn and sent her aloft. Flying through the air, she didn't know what to do. To the instincts inside her, she had to be true. Roslyn wrapped herself around a tree growing out of a crag. Because of her weight, the tree started to sag.

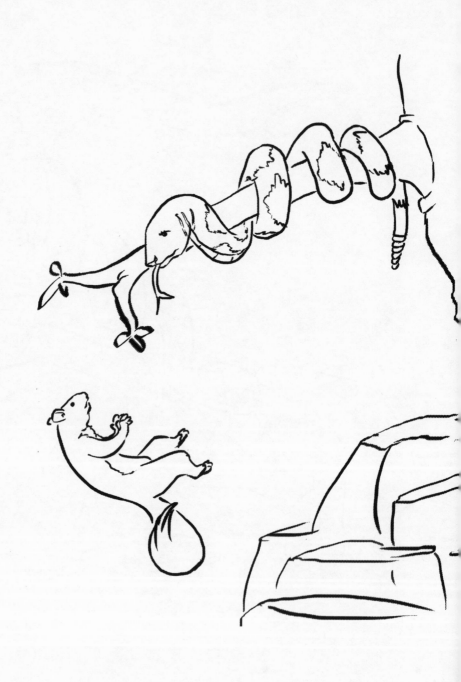

Weasel was hungry and angry as he could be. He jumped out to nab Roslyn as she clung to the tree. One claw scrapped Roslyn's back and gave her a wound. Weasel missed latching on and fell to his doom.

When Roslyn finished trembling, she made it to safety. She never fully realized how she'd acted so bravely. She lay there exhausted on top of a flat red rock. She couldn't even move because she was in shock. Roslyn realized she couldn't give up; she had to survive. She had weathered one of life's storms, now happy to be alive.

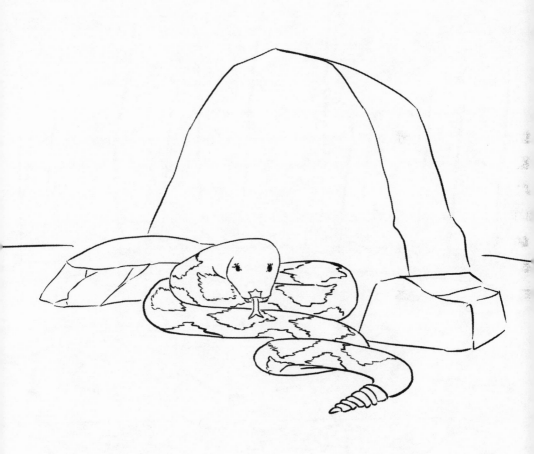

The hot summer wind turned into a cool autumn breeze. The season was changing, and so were the leaves. Bright reds, oranges, and yellows fell to the forest floor. Roslyn turned her thoughts to brumation and considered death no more. Roslyn's body was heavy as her belly continued to swell. She knew she must do something as the temperatures fell. It was getting cold as the sun sunk low in the storm-laden sky. She had to find shelter and wasn't certain why.

Roslyn found the entrance to a very small cave. It looked very scary, but she had to be brave. Roslyn slithered inside, and what did she find? A snake named Mary, who was so very kind.

"Lie here among us to escape the winter storm," said Mary. "We must lie here for warmth and take sanctuary. In the spring, we give birth to the babes we all carry. For all of us mother rattlesnakes, it is customary."

Roslyn saw thousands of snakes on the dark cave floor. She wandered outside in the harsh winter no more. Beneath the ground, Roslyn found warmth and safety. She snuggled in among the snakes and got so comfy.

Snowflakes fell, and the cold wind piled snow into a drift. Something moved inside Roslyn, so her body had to shift. Thousands of rattlesnakes were hiding out from the storm. In the forest, the deer pawed the ground for food but couldn't keep warm. The pond where Roslyn and Rico had met was now frozen over. Drifts of white snow covered the green field of clover.

Roslyn dreamed of the little snakes that grew in her womb. Certainly they'd survive the storms of life, she had to assume. Roslyn dreamed of a handsome snake and thought she'd known love. She couldn't remember his name. Was he sent from above? Roslyn dreamed of a monster who brought nightmarish terror. She knew that she'd faced one to survive, but was it in error?

Changes went on inside Roslyn's body—of that, there was no doubt. Very soon, it would be time for the babes incubating inside Roslyn to come out.

The cold snows of winter warmed into the cool rains of spring. The robins came back and started to sing. Roslyn left the cave and found a place for privacy. She found a cleft in a rock that was near a pine tree.

Nestled snug on a bed of grass and some weeds, Roslyn gave birth to her neonates, fulfilling life's needs. A dozen tiny snakes flowed from Roslyn's starved body. It seemed to Roslyn this was what life should embody. As the temperatures climbed and the snows started to melt, Roslyn came to appreciate this life she'd been dealt. Roslyn knew someone must be there to design her life's plan. Now she was fulfilled, surrounded by her clan.

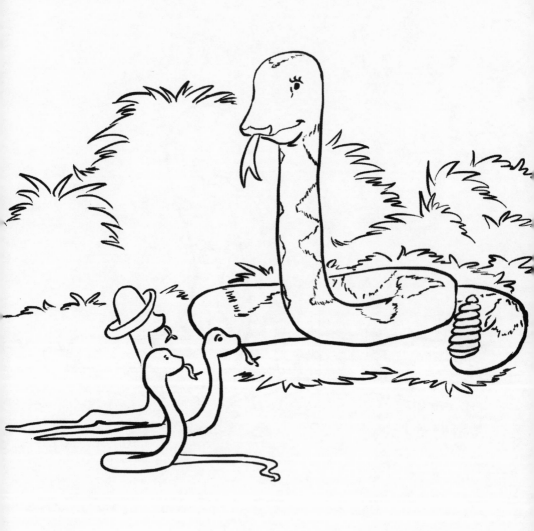

Roslyn told her neonates, "Life is full of dangers and challenges to face. Go through your lives with courage, and each day embrace. There really is meaning to everything you do. Just remember who you are, and to your own self be true. You were born to be rattlesnakes to hunt the forest floor. So go forth and prosper. Life's full of wonders to explore."

As each neonate set off on its own adventure, Roslyn realized that caring for another was life's true treasure. The future was full of shadows impossible to see. So Roslyn embraced being a rattlesnake and did so joyfully.